Up

Joe Cepeda

HOLIDAY HOUSE / NEW YORK

For the Licanos

Copyright © 2016 by Joe Cepeda
All Rights Reserved
HOLIDAY HOUSE is registered in the U.S. Patent and Trademark Office.
Printed and bound in April 2016 at Tien Wah Press, Johor Bahru, Johor, Malaysia.
The artwork was created with digital tools.
www.holidayhouse.com
First Edition
1 3 5 7 9 10 8 6 4 2
Library of Congress Cataloging-in-Publication Data

Names: Cepeda, Joe, author, illustrator.
Title: Up / Joe Cepeda.
Description: First edition. | New York : Holiday House, [2016] | Series: I
like to read | Summary: "On a very windy day, a boy stands by a window
with his pinwheel and is suddenly whisked into the sky where he can see a
pig, a hen, a cow, and a sheep"— Provided by publisher.
Identifiers: LCCN 2015045420 | ISBN 9780823436552 (hardcover)
Subjects: | CYAC: Winds—Fiction. | Domestic animals—Fiction.
Classification: LCC PZ7.C3184 Up 2016 | DDC [E]—dc23 LC record available at http://lccn.loc.gov/2015045420
ISBN 978-0-8234-3689-7 (paperback)

Look.

Look.

I go up.

I see a hen.

I see a sheep.

I see a cow.

I see a pig.

They go home.

I go home.